Summit at the Sleepy Inn

Written by Stella Santa Cruz
Illustrated by Gaston Vanzet

Contents

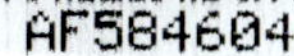

Meet the Characters

Aunty Rita

The owner of the Sleepy Inn.

President Findlay

President of the USA.

Premier Qing Xuan

Premier of China.

Dear Reader

I once stayed at a motel in rural Australia that had dozens of signs everywhere telling me what NOT to do. I had a lot of fun disobeying most of them. One day, while I was there, I wondered what would happen if some really important people came to stay. Would they be expected to behave as well?

Stella Santa Cruz
Author

The Sleepy Inn, Fairhaven

1. The Sleepy Inn motel
2. Fairhaven aerodrome
3. The wharf
4. Grandad Perkins' Takeaway and Bait Shop

1 Breaking the Rules

Aunty Rita's tongue curled up the side of her mouth and moved slowly across her flamingo-pink lips. It was a sure sign that she was involved in an important task requiring the utmost attention.

When she had finished her important task, she balanced her reading glasses on her nose, and prepared to admire her handiwork.

"NO RUNNIGN!" read Aunty Rita, wrinkling up her nose in disappointment at the sign she had just written. "That's not right," she muttered. "Bother!"

She found another piece of cardboard and, once more, the tip of her tongue crept out of her mouth. Finally, she sat back and peered at her lettering with narrowed eyes, as if that would somehow correct any further spelling mistakes.

"Ah," she said, pursing her lipstick-laden lips victoriously. "That's better. NO RUNNING."

NO RUNNING

Aunty Rita had a firm belief in rules and regulations and, since she had taken over the Sleepy Inn motel, she had written down plenty of them – all on cardboard signs, scattered abundantly around the cabins, play areas and pathways.

Aunty Rita liked her guests to be well behaved and she suspected that if there weren't signs around the Sleepy Inn, guests would spend their entire holiday deliberately running everywhere, walking on the grass, bouncing balls, sitting on chairs with wet swimmers, doing forward rolls on the trampoline or recklessly changing channels in the TV room.

Aunty Rita scooped a handful of drawing pins into her palm and tucked the new sign under her arm. She headed out of her office and past the reception desk, which was laden with brochures, small key rings saying "I've Been Driven to Fairhaven" and brightly coloured fishing lines for sale. She headed towards the swimming pool area.

She noticed the Hendersons, who had just checked in with their family of three children, heading in the same direction with rolled up towels under their arms. She

picked up her pace and, with a triumphant grin, arrived at the pool area just ahead of the Hendersons.

Tongue peeping between her lips, she fixed her new sign to the changing room door and stood back, knowing she had just removed another opportunity for misbehaviour with seconds to spare.

"Hello!" she said cheerily to the Hendersons.

"Hello," they called back. They headed for the changing rooms and stopped, peering at the new sign.

"Phew," breathed Aunty Rita to herself. "Just in the nick of time!"

She trotted primly back towards her office, satisfied with a job well done.

Sixteen thousand, four hundred and ten kilometres away, the red, top-secret emergency telephone in the White House's Oval Office rang.

President Findlay, who had been holding an emergency crisis meeting with Kryzinski, his Chief of Staff, and his top advisors, sat behind his desk, looking exhausted. He and the other men and women in the White House had been awake for 36 hours without a moment's sleep. They had found themselves dealing with a major international crisis.

The phone continued ringing insistently. Everyone in the Oval Office knew who would be calling. Kryzinski glanced nervously towards the president.

"I guess that's for me," joked President Findlay, without a trace of humour in his gravelly voice. No one laughed. The phone rang again. President Findlay sighed and reached resignedly for the receiver.

"Good evening, Mr Premier," he said, looking at his watch. "Or I should say 'good morning'. It's Sunday night here, but Monday morning there, I believe."

"And by the time you Americans reach Monday morning, you will realise just how much trouble the world will be in very soon," crackled Premier Qing Xuan's voice impatiently. "In this country, we do not take kindly to people shooting down our meteorological satellites!"

"And, Mr Premier, in this country we do not appreciate people taking detailed satellite photographs of the weather above our military bases. Especially when it occurs three times a day and usually when there's not a cloud in sight."

"Nonsense," replied the premier emphatically. "We are perfectly entitled to see if there are storm clouds gathering on the other side of the Pacific."

"And are there, Mr Premier?" challenged the president, trying to disguise the tiredness in his voice.

"No," replied the premier. "But there are some very dark clouds forming on our side of the Pacific. You should be warned that they are heading your way."

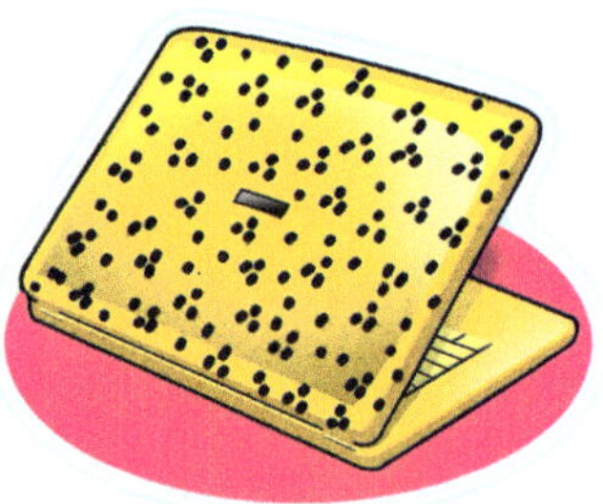

Aunty Rita sat in her office, peering intently at the computer screen in front of her.

"Build your own website!" declared the Internet advertisement she had clicked on. "It couldn't be easier. And your subscription is free for the first year!"

Aunty Rita pushed her reading glasses up her nose, licked her lips and, with her tongue wandering across her mouth, she started typing.

"Sleepy Inn Motel," she typed. She shook her head and hit the backspace button, erasing the word "Motel".

"Sleepy Inn Resort," she keyed in, pressing the final "t" with a dramatic flourish. That sounded much better. "Fairhaven's Premier Destination!"

That was certainly true, she reflected. It was the premier destination because, after all, the Sleepy Inn was Fairhaven's only destination. Unless, of course, you counted Grandad Perkins' Takeaway and Bait Shop. But you couldn't sleep there. Not longer than the twenty minutes it took for Grandad Perkins to deep-fry your piece of fish and scoop of chips, anyway.

A message flashed up on Aunty Rita's computer screen. "Insert photograph," it prompted helpfully. "Upload your own image or use our free photo library."

"Oh dear," said Aunty Rita. "I don't have any photographs of the Sleepy Inn." She clicked on the button that said "Complimentary Photo Library" and pored over the selection of beautiful tropical beach resort photos that she found there.

"Ooh, that looks nice," she said to herself, finding a glorious photograph of a deckchair on a long stretch of white sandy beach, ringed with palm trees. Over a beautiful tropical lagoon, the sun was setting, casting a golden glow over the scene.

"There is an old eucalyptus tree down by the wharf," thought Aunty Rita. "Once the sun sets and it's dark, you would hardly notice the difference between that and a palm tree!"

She selected the image.

"Tick amenities," suggested the computer on the next window. Aunty Rita scrolled through a list of resort amenities.

"Conference facilities?" enquired the computer politely. Aunty Rita thought hard. The ping-pong table could certainly be used as a conference table, she thought. She ticked the box.

"Private bathrooms?" asked the computer. Aunty Rita gleefully ticked the box. She had just repaired all the doors in the toilet block, so it was quite private now.

"Luxury spa facilities?" probed the computer. Aunty Rita thought for a moment. On a really hot summer's day, the hot tub next to the laundry room was quite comfortable, even though it wasn't actually connected to the hot water.

"WiFi?" asked the computer. Aunty Rita wrinkled her nose, wondering what on earth that was supposed to mean. WiFi? It did smell a little bit unpleasant when the tide went out and the mudflats started to heat up in the sun, but she'd call it more "squiffy" than "wifi". She decided, however, it was always best to be honest, and ticked the box.

"Golf?" was the next option. "Number of holes?"

Aunty Rita made a tsk-tsk sound. She'd asked her handyperson Dennis to repair the minigolf area, but there were still holes all over the artificial lawn. She ticked the biggest number she could find, which was 36.

Her finger hovered ovcr thc "Next" box, but suddenly, with a loud *ping*, the bell on the reception desk interrupted Aunty Rita's concentration. She jumped in alarm, and accidentally pushed the "Publish" button at the top of her computer screen. She craned her head around the office door, and saw Mr Henderson standing in reception looking glumly at the fishing lines for sale on the corner of the desk.

"Could we have some soap, please?" he asked.

"Goodness!" said Aunty Rita, bustling out to the desk and rustling around in a cardboard box of soap bars. "Are they gone already? I changed thosc bars only three weeks ago," she said. "I need to make some new signs for the shower block." She picked out a bar of soap. "No wasting soap," she murmured thoughtfully. "Yes, that should do it."

2 A Reservation

Something loud and annoying was intent on interrupting President Findlay's dream. He groaned. It had been almost two days since he had been to bed, and now that he had finally crawled between his comfortable White House sheets, something was waking him up from his deep sleep.

Buzz, buzz went the telephone next to the presidential bed. *Buzz, buzz.*

President Findlay groped for the receiver.

"Hello?" he yawned, unable to prise his eyes open. It was one of his advisors. He was babbling something urgently at the president, who was still struggling to wake himself up.

"Is it Saturday yet?" he mumbled, yawning again. "All I want is to sleep in. Sleep in."

"I'll see to it, Mr President," confirmed the advisor and the telephone line went dead. President Findlay flopped his head back onto the fluffy grey presidential pillows, exhausted. Within seconds, the president was fast asleep again.

Aunty Rita's tongue was working overtime. There were five showers in the shower block, and each one of them would require a sign informing guests of the Sleepy Inn's new Soap Usage Regulation. The smell of fresh marker pen wafted out of the office door.

Just as Aunty Rita was about to finish the fifth sign with an exclamation mark, the telephone on her desk rang loudly. She jumped, inadvertently turning the full stop into an alarmed squiggle.

"Bother!" said Aunty Rita in exasperation. She capped her marker pen and picked up the phone.

"Yes?" she said, wondering who was interrupting her important sign writing.

"Is this the Sleepy Inn Resort?" came a busy-sounding voice.

"Yes, dear," said Aunty Rita. She tossed the cardboard sign in the bin and picked up another sheet from her desk.

"Yes, dear," she said again, as she listened to the voice. "Yes, I think we have a vacancy." She ran her finger down the wall calendar and rested it upon Saturday.

Aunty Rita scribbled a few notes as the voice asked more questions.

"International cuisine, dear?" said Aunty Rita. She thought for a moment. Grandad Perkins' Takeaway and Bait Shop did serve dim sums, she remembered.

"Yes, dear," nodded Aunty Rita. Then, just as the caller was about to hang up, she had a thought.

"Will you be wanting soap, dear?"

There was a surprised silence on the other end of the line.

"Er, yes, I imagine we will require soap," said the caller.

"Just checking, dear," said Aunty Rita. The line went dead and Aunty Rita picked up her marker pen with renewed vigour. If the entire Sleepy Inn was to be booked out for the weekend, she'd definitely need signs for all of the shower cubicles! And signs warning people not to waste toilet paper in the toilet block probably wouldn't hurt either.

Aunty Rita reached for a thick sheaf of cardboard sheets, readied her tongue for some intense concentration and readjusted her reading glasses determinedly. This was going to be a busy afternoon.

3 Check-In Time

"The Chinese will be flying in shortly, Mr President," said Kryzinski as the presidential party prepared to disembark from the United States presidential jet, Air Force One.

Secret arrangements between all three governments had meant that the president and the premier were able to slip into the country unnoticed, even though the Australians had sounded a little surprised at the unusual choice of venue for an international crisis meeting.

President Findlay adjusted his expensive silk tie and stepped out of the aircraft. A small flag fluttered in the breeze above the tiny aerodrome.

"Welcome to Fairhaven", it said, "Radish Capital of Bairnsley County". The president stared at the large faded plastic radish that stood proudly above the aerodrome roof.

"This is going to be interesting," he murmured. He'd attended international conferences and secret diplomatic meetings all around the world, but he'd never yet struck a "radish capital".

Welcome to Fairhaven
Radish Capital of Bairnsley County

"Sir, the presidential motorcade is waiting," said Kryzinski.

Minutes later, the president and his advisors, accompanied by a handful of secret service agents in dark glasses, were bumping their way towards Fairhaven.

Aunty Rita finished folding the ends of the toilet rolls into small triangles. Then she sprayed the interior of the toilet block liberally with tropical mangrove and raspberry air freshener, her favourite.

One of the Henderson boys ran into the toilet block and skidded to a halt the moment he saw Aunty Rita. She waggled her finger pointedly towards a "No Running" sign that was affixed firmly to the door of the block.

"Sorry," said the boy sheepishly. "Pooh! What's that smell? Is it fly spray?"

The chauffeur of the limousine at the front of the motorcade braked suddenly. The gravel road in front of the car had come to an end. He looked around, puzzled.

The secret service agents in the following car felt for their weapons nervously. They were not used to being on deserted roads. Was this an ambush?

"Surely that wasn't it?" whispered the chauffeur to Kryzinski, who was sitting in the front seat with him. "That rickety old shop and that deserted petrol station a few kilometres back?"

Kryzinski shrugged. "Maybe it was," he said.

The chauffeur pressed the radio button on the dashboard and delivered a few urgent directions to the vehicle behind. Both limousines pulled over to the side and attempted to manoeuvre around on the thin, gravelly road. It took quite a few minutes of driving backwards and forwards before they could head back towards Fairhaven.

Back at Fairhaven Aerodrome, Qing Xuan stepped briskly down the steps of the Chinese air force jet that had parked a respectable distance from the blue and

white Air Force One. He looked around, a slight frown on his face. He was used to being greeted by a military guard of honour or a row of diplomats. Instead, there was a lone disinterested crow preening itself on the tarmac.

Craaw went the crow.

Qing Xuan's foreign minister, Wei-Lun Chiu, stepped down beside the premier.

"The Americans promised there would be a limousine motorcade," he hissed angrily.

"Maybe they're just late getting here," replied Qing Xuan. "They did say they would take Findlay and his advisors to the resort if they arrived first."

He stared at the curiously shaped faded plastic object atop the aerodrome building.

"It looks like a high-security satellite listening device," warned Wei-Lun Chiu in a low voice. "We should be careful what we say."

After Grandad Perkins had given a secret service agent directions, the motorcade finally arrived at the Sleepy Inn.

Hearing the crunch of tyres upon gravel, Aunty Rita finished the last sign outlining the "Maximum Five Squares Per Person" toilet paper policy and headed for the reception desk.

"Good morning," she said, while smiling at the serious-looking men in reception. One of the men spoke.

"Good morning, ma'am," he said. "My name is Kryzinski. Do you have the keys to our rooms?"

"Of course, dear," said Aunty Rita. "But I'll just fill this in first," she smiled, tapping a registration form with a pencil. "Name?"

Kryzinski's face clouded over.

"Archibald Findlay, President of the United States of America," he said in disbelief.

"That's OK, dear, I don't need an occupation," said Aunty Rita, her tongue waggling in unison with the pencil scribbling on the card. "Number plate?"

"What?" said Kryzinski.

"How did you get here, dear?" asked Aunty Rita patiently. "We don't want to get towed away, now, do we?"

"AIR FORCE ONE!" blustered Kryzinski.

Aunty Rita shook her head as she wrote down the registration number. Personalised plates. Everyone was getting them these days.

"Home address, dear?" enquired Aunty Rita.

"The White House, 1600 Pennsylvania Avenue, Washington, DC, 20500," sighed Kryzinski.

"Oh, I do prefer white houses, dear," said Aunty Rita. "They always look so much crisper and tidier, don't you think?"

Premier Qing Xuan and Foreign Minister Wei-Lun Chiu remained standing at attention at the bottom of the steps of the Chinese jet.

"Do you think we should move into the shade, Your Excellency?" asked Wei-Lun. "It is very hot."

"That would be a sign of weakness and informality," replied Qing Xuan resolutely. "We will remain here in full sunlight."

Wei-Lun Chiu wiped a bead of perspiration from his brow. Fortunately, at that moment, the long bonnet

of a limousine appeared around the corner of the aerodrome. The motorcade had made its way back to the tarmac. The cars accelerated towards the Chinese party and the lone crow took to the air with an irritated *craaw.*

The Chinese leaders got into the limousines. One of the Chinese advisors got into the front seat where Kryzinski had sat half an hour earlier.

"You're not going to believe this," grinned the chauffeur, shaking his head.

"Believe what?" asked the advisor, raising her eyebrows.

4 Enjoy the Facilities!

The president and the premier eyed each other suspiciously over the ping-pong table.

The advisors who stood by the ping-pong table tried to look serious and stern, but it was difficult while the sound of Aunty Rita's washing machine next door whirred noisily into spin cycle.

"Very cunning!" accused Wei-Lun Chiu. "You bring us to a backwater because you are too embarrassed to negotiate anywhere else!"

"You asked the president to nominate a neutral place and he did," retorted Kryzinski defiantly.

"Did I?" whispered President Findlay. "I thought you booked this place."

"You ... oh, never mind," replied Kryzinski. "We're here now."

Qing Xuan coughed, and Wei-Lun Chiu barked an order at one of the advisors. She hopped up instantly and raced for the door.

"The destruction of our meteorological satellite must have very serious consequences," said the Chinese premier.

"That was an act of aggression against the peace-loving people of China who were merely protecting their security."

"I thought you said it was a weather satellite," replied President Findlay firmly. "Are your people peace loving or sunshine loving?"

"Excuse me, young lady!"

The Chinese advisor stopped in her tracks and turned around in alarm.

Standing with her arms folded, Aunty Rita nodded towards a "No Running" sign stuck onto the laundry door.

"I am getting some water for Premier Xuan," explained the advisor breathlessly.

"So next you'll be running with a glass of water, dear?" said Aunty Rita, shaking her head. "Oh, no, dear, that won't do. What if you fall over and hurt yourself?"

“I am a Fujian White Crane expert in Shaolin boxing, tai chi chuan and kung fu!” said the advisor in astonishment.

“That’s very nice, dear,” said Aunty Rita, “but if you look on the reception wall, you’ll see that I have a certificate from the Bairnsley Community College in Safe Laundry Practices, and you don’t get one of those by running with a glass of water in your hand!”

“But ...” said the advisor.

Aunty Rita waggled a stern finger at the woman. “You just turn around, young lady, and walk sensibly. I’ll bring a pitcher of water over to the ping-pong room for you and your friends.”

The door to the ping-pong room, or the conference suite as it was now, burst open. The two delegations turned their glowering stares towards the doorway. But, instead of the young Chinese advisor, they found themselves staring in surprise at the Henderson family.

"Do you think you'll be long?" asked Mrs Henderson.

"I promised the kids a game of ping-pong after lunch," explained Mr Henderson with a smile.

"Wow!" said one of the boys, looking at all the delegates around the table. "I've heard of doubles, but this is even bigger than triples or quadruples, Dad. Can we watch?"

"Come on, boys," said Mrs Henderson, bustling the children out of the room. "Let's go and wait on the end of the wharf until they've finished their game."

"Can we get some fishing lines?" asked one of the boys. "They have them at reception!"

"OK," smiled Mr Henderson. He waved at the people surrounding the ping-pong table. "Sorry," he said. "We'll come back later."

By the time the sun had started to set that day, the Hendersons had given up all hope of fitting in a game of ping-pong before dinner. The two delegations had given up all hope of reaching an agreement, and Kryzinski

had suggested they get some dinner and an early night. That was the one thing that both sides agreed upon.

"Eight cheeseburgers, six scoops of chips and thirty-two dim sums?" said Grandad Perkins, not sure he'd heard correctly. He didn't know if he had that much food in the refrigerator.

"That's right," nodded the chauffeur, who had been sent down to organise dinner. "And sixteen bottles of soda."

"What?" said a bewildered Grandad Perkins.

The chauffeur whispered something into the microphone hidden in his sleeve and, back at the Sleepy Inn, one of the secret service agents consulted his top-secret CIA handbook. The chauffeur's earpiece crackled as the secret service agent replied to the chauffeur's request.

"I'm told you call it fizzy drink here," said the chauffeur, smiling.

"No, we call it fizzy drink everywhere," said Grandad Perkins, hunting fruitlessly through the fridge for an extra box of dim sums. "I can do twenty-four dim sums and sixteen spring rolls," he declared. "Will that do?"

The chauffeur nodded.

“More orders tonight than I’ve had in a month,” grumbled Grandad Perkins as he filled a deep-fryer basket with food. “Now I’ve completely run out of every kind of food.”

The doorbell clanged as the door to Grandad Perkins’ Takeaway and Bait Shop opened.

“Hello!” grinned Mr Henderson, as he and his family walked into the shop. “We’ve been hanging out for those delicious dim sums of yours all day! Hope you’ve got enough to feed a hungry family!”

5 Do Not Disturb

Premier Qing Xuan tossed and turned restlessly. He'd been trying to get to sleep for what seemed like hours. But his mind was racing and he kept burping up a most undiplomatic mixture that smelled of stale dim sum mixed with deep-fried spring roll.

He reached over and turned on the bedside light. He gazed at the ceiling of the log cabin that was serving as the official residence of the premier of the People's Republic of China for the night. Its timber frames and simple furnishings reminded him of the house he and his brothers and sisters had grown up in years ago beside the banks of the winding Jialing River.

He swung himself out of bed, knowing that it was pointless trying to get to sleep.

He remembered how he and his siblings used to sometimes clamber out the window of their old family house and walk beside the moonlit river at night. He smiled nostalgically.

"Those were good days, Qing," he said to himself.

"No international incidents to sort out. No military stand-offs. Nothing but enjoying myself with my friends and family."

Outside, a moth owl called.

"I'm going for a walk," decided the premier. "Maybe that will help me to sleep."

He pulled on his slippers and a dressing gown and silently opened the door, careful not to wake the rest of the Chinese delegation in the neighbouring cabins.

Outside, the air was warm and gently scented by the eucalyptus trees that were scattered about the grounds of the Sleepy Inn. The moth owl called again and Qing Xuan turned his head to see if he could spot the bird. He peered down the track out to the wharf. Then, as his eyes adjusted to the dark, he stiffened. There, sitting on the edge of the wharf, was a lone figure. Premier Qing Xuan had seen that figure often enough to know exactly who it was, even in silhouette. He stood and watched in silence.

President Findlay pulled the lapels of his dressing gown up around his neck. It was a warm night, but the breeze blowing down the estuary and swirling around the wooden poles of the wharf was cool. In the darkness, a fish splashed as it caught an insect floating on top of the dark water. In the distance, the moth owl called again.

He heard footsteps approaching and sighed. No matter how hard he tried to elude them, the secret service agents seemed to have a knack for keeping track of the president's whereabouts.

"Sorry," he said quietly. "I should have told you, but I just couldn't sleep."

The footsteps stopped behind him.

"Me neither," said a voice that definitely did not belong to a secret service agent. The president whirled around and found himself staring at the Chinese premier.

"Do you mind?" asked Qing Xuan, indicating the edge of the wharf next to the president.

"Not at all," replied Findlay. "Have a seat."

The world's two most powerful politicians sat silently in their dressing gowns, legs dangling over the edge of the wharf, wondering what they should say to each other. Finally, the premier spoke.

"This reminds me of when I was a young boy," he said softly. "The river. The stars. The call of the night birds."

The president nodded. "I was just thinking much the same thing," he said. "Do you know this is the first time since becoming president that I've been out at night, completely alone with nothing but my thoughts?"

The premier nodded. In the distance, another fish broke the water with a splash.

"There's plenty out there," observed the president.

"That's why I borrowed these," grinned the premier, drawing a pair of fishing lines from inside his dressing gown. "I'll let you have one, as long as you don't tell Aunty Rita that it was me who took them without paying."

The president grinned. "I haven't fished off a wharf since I was ten years old!" he said with a look of childish delight. "Don't suppose you've got any bait?"

"I have a leftover dim sum," chuckled the premier.

"That'll be sure to scare off all the fish," said the president.

"Catching fish is not the purpose of fishing," observed the premier wisely. "Fishing is the purpose of fishing."

"Only a fisher would understand that," agreed the president, slipping half a dim sum onto his hook. There were two plops, as the lines dropped into the dark waters. The two men sat in silence, watching the dappled moonlight reflected on the surface of the water.

Suddenly, President Findlay clambered to his feet.

"I've got a bite!" he said urgently. He tugged tentatively on his fishing line and something on the other end gave a sharp tug back. "I think I've got one!"

Premier Qing Xuan stood up and peered eagerly over the water. There was a sudden splash and the premier pointed excitedly. "He's a big one!" he said, nodding at the president. "Haul in your line."

The president, who felt like an excited boy again, wound the fishing line around the reel as fast as he could. Suddenly, the line went slack.

"Oh, no," said the president. "I think ..."

"No!" cried the premier enthusiastically. "He's just swimming this way. Pull in your line. Quicker!"

The president wound up the line and, within a few seconds, felt another sharp tug.

"He's back!" he called, another grin lighting up his face.

"Watch out!" called the premier, who was leaning out, trying to get a glimpse of the fish in the waters below. "He's heading for the piles of the wharf. Don't let him get ... AAAH!"

The president looked up in alarm, just in time to see the premier of the People's Republic of China toppling off the wharf.

He dropped the fishing line and desperately lurched towards a flailing arm. He caught the sleeve of the premier's dressing gown but, in doing so, he overbalanced himself.

"WHOAH!" cried the president, as he felt the weight of the Chinese premier pull him off the wharf.

SPLASH! SPLASH!

For a second, President Findlay was disoriented, as his nostrils and mouth filled with salty estuary water.

He scrambled around in the water, then felt something soft. His hand grasped onto the object and he pulled himself upright.

He discovered it was the premier's dressing gown. And the premier himself was standing waist deep in the water, laughing with a deep, rumbling belly laugh.

The president smiled. He looked around. And then he started to laugh too. Soon, the estuary echoed with roars of laughter, as the world's two most powerful politicians sloshed their way out of the water and across the mudflats.

"That was the funniest thing to happen to me for years," guffawed President Findlay.

"I haven't laughed like this since I moved to Beijing," gasped Premier Qing Xuan. The two men trudged up the pathway to the Sleepy Inn, leaving a trail of wet splashes and footprints behind them.

"In here," said President Findlay, pointing to the ping-pong room. "Let's heat up some of that coffee we had left over from today's meeting."

Premier Qing Xuan sat on one of the chairs, chuckling to himself, while President Findlay switched

on the coffee machine. He came back and drew up a chair next to the premier.

"You know, let's just forget about this whole satellite thing," he said. "We'll cover the cost of replacing it, as long as you guys don't fly over our air force bases. We aren't doing anything you need to know about."

Premier Qing Xuan looked appreciatively at President Findlay and nodded. He opened his mouth to speak – when suddenly the door of the ping-pong room swung open.

The president and the premier turned around, expecting to see a bevy of irate advisors and secret service agents searching for their leaders.

Instead, they saw an irate Aunty Rita staring at them accusingly.

"Now, boys," she said, putting her hands squarely on her hips. "Do I have to spell this out for you?"

The president and the premier glanced at each other like two naughty boys who had just been caught doing something they shouldn't.

"Spell what out, Aunty Rita?" asked the premier, trying to suppress a giggle.

Aunty Rita took a sharp breath, and pointed towards a sign on the wall.

"NO SITTING ON CHAIRS WITH WET SWIMMERS!" instructed the sign.

Aunty Rita pursed her lips and narrowed her eyes. "And I don't suppose either of you would know anything about two missing fishing lines, would you?"

"No, Aunty Rita," said the president, looking at the floor nervously.

"No, Aunty Rita," echoed the premier, jiggling sheepishly from one foot to the other.

"Hmm," said Aunty Rita. "I didn't think so." She whirled around and went back to reception, shaking her head and muttering something about rules and how no one takes any notice these days.

6 Slippery Soap

The peaceful isolation of the Sleepy Inn was exactly what the world needed. The world's two most powerful leaders rediscovered the things that were really important: enjoying the songs of the birds, breathing in the fresh air, and watching the world go by from the end of a sun-soaked, rickety old wharf.

They also discovered that they were not enemies, but could enjoy each other's company. And that, sometimes, breaking Aunty Rita's rules could be fun.

"Oh, bad luck!" shouted the Chinese premier, with a glint in his eye. He lined up his shot and gently swung the battered golf putter he was holding.

The president watched ruefully as the premier's ball wobbled its way up the minigolf ramp, and clattered noisily into the hole that the president had aimed for and missed.

"That must be China three, United States nil!" crowed the premier, beaming at the president.

"No, that would be ..." started Kryzinski from the sidelines. The president waved at him to be quiet.

"OK, Qing. So you beat me at minigolf. Once those Henderson kids get off the conference table, I'm going to whip you at ping-pong!" he said cheekily.

"An American president whipping a Chinese premier at ping-pong?" winked the premier incredulously. "No way!"

"In the meantime, I say we should have a go on that trampoline," suggested the president.

Kryzinski and Wei-Lun Chiu looked at each other in total bewilderment. Overnight, the president and the premier seemed to have solved all the problems of the world and were acting like they were best buddies.

"I'm just glad to see you all playing together nicely and behaving like you should," piped up Aunty Rita, who had been knitting in one of the deckchairs to the side of the minigolf course. "I know everyone pooh-poohs my rules, but without rules no one will get along," she said.

"I guess so, ma'am," shrugged Kryzinski. "Well, we've achieved our purpose. We've avoided the slippery slope to international conflict."

Aunty Rita's ears pricked up, and a frown crossed her face. "Slippery soap?" she said, pursing her flamingo-pink lips in dismay.

"Now don't tell me you've run out of that already," she said, shaking her head in disbelief.

"Really, dear," she harrumphed resignedly. "I don't know why no one reads my signs!"

AVAILABLE NOW! Selected suites at the world-famous Sleepy Inn Motel. Group bookings welcome!

Morning News

HUNGRY? Family pack 50 wontons plus fizzy drink NOW at Grandad Perkins' Takeaway and Bait Shop!

50 c

TODAY'S EDITION

N.1

SUPERPOWERS SIGN FRIENDSHIP AGREEMENT

A joint announcement from the President of the United States and the Premier of the People's Republic of China revealed a new friendship agreement between the two superpowers. The agreement, negotiated at an undisclosed location, has several peculiar clauses, including "no arguing", "no wasting satellites", and some

Sleepy Inn
Motel
International
Summit Centre
NO ARGUING!